WHO ARE YOU?

BY
DAVID ORME

ILLUSTRATED BY
SEB CAMAGAJEVAC

Titles in the Full Flight Heroes and Heroines series:

Who Are You?	David Orme
3Dee	Danny Pearson
Doom Clone	Melanie Joyce
Too Risky!	Alison Hawes
Wanda Darkstar	Jane A C West
Galactic Games: Sci-Fi Spy Guy	Roger Hurn
Robot Eyes	Jillian Powell
Charlie's Tin	Lynda Gore
Run For Your Life	Jonny Zucker

Badger Publishing Limited
Oldmedow Road,
Hardwick Industrial Estate,
King's Lynn PE30 4JJ
Telephone: 01438 791037
www.badgerlearning.co.uk

2 4 6 8 10 9 7 5 3 1

Who Are You? ISBN 978 1 84926 482 2

Text © David Orme 2011
Complete work © Badger Publishing Limited 2011
Second edition © 2014

The right of David Orme to be identified as author of this Work
has been asserted by him in accordance with the Copyright,
Designs and Patents Act 1988.

Badger Publishing would like to thank Jonny Zucker for his help
in putting this series together.

Publisher: David Jamieson
Senior Editor: Danny Pearson
Design: Fiona Grant
Illustration: Seb Camagajevac

CONTENTS

New words:

identical   survivors

opposite   unusual

wreckage   attendant

Main characters:

Gemma

Becky

CHAPTER 1
Bumpy Landing

"This is the captain speaking. We shall be landing at London Gatwick in ten minutes. Please fasten your seatbelts. There is a thunderstorm at the moment and landing may be a little bumpy."

Gemma and Becky Clarke looked at each other. Gemma knew that Becky really hated this bit!

The twin girls were coming home. They had been staying with their aunt and uncle in Texas. Although the girls were twins, they were very different.

Becky was shy and nervous, and hated take-off and landing. Gemma was quite the opposite.

Gemma held her sister's hand tightly. "We'll be down soon," she whispered. "Just hang on in there, Becky!"

Becky just nodded. She thought she might be sick if she tried to speak.

Outside the plane, there was a flash of lightning. The passengers could hear the crash of thunder even above the noise of the engines.

The plane bounced up and down. Becky's face was looking very green.

The captain spoke again.

"Don't worry, It feels worse than it is! Once we're through the clouds it will be smoother. Landing in five minutes."

It was too much for Becky. She reached for the sick bag and opened it just in time.

There wasn't much that Gemma could do to help. She looked straight ahead. You didn't feel so sick if you did that.

The plane suddenly lurched from side to side. Then came a horrible moment when it seemed to be falling straight down. Becky groaned and was sick again.

The front of the plane tilted downwards. The angle got steeper and steeper. Too steep! Becky felt the seat belt cutting into her.

The engines roared. Lightning flashed around the plane. Terrified passengers were screaming, screaming . . .

CHAPTER 2
Where Are They?

A frightened farm worker was the only person who actually saw the crash. He had been standing at a barn door, sheltering from the rain.

He heard an aircraft low overhead. This wasn't unusual as the farm was right next to the airport. This time, though, the noise was louder, as if the plane was much lower than usual.

The roar of its engines got even louder. The sound was deafening.

For an instant he saw the fat nose of a big jet coming down through the clouds.

Then there was an explosion that seemed to go on and on. The ground shook. The farm worker was almost knocked off his feet.

The emergency services were on the spot in minutes. A helicopter flew low overhead. The pilot looked down in horror. Wreckage was spread across the whole field. Black smoke was rising from a burning section of the plane.

No one could have survived.

Jeff Turner, the fire chief, dreaded the job he had to do. Clearing up after a major air crash must be the worst job in the world.

His team started work, putting out the fire and searching for anyone who might still be alive.

It didn't take long to realise the incredible truth.

The plane was smashed into a million pieces. But there wasn't a body to be found.

***

On the other side of the world, Bob Cummings, a sheep farmer in Western Australia, had just finished his breakfast. He heard a bang on his door.

Who on Earth could that be?

He didn't get many visitors. His nearest neighbours were miles away!

At the door stood two girls. Two girls with the same face. Identical twins.

Chapter 3
Are They Human?

The investigation into the crash wasn't going well. In a top secret building in London, a group of men and women were sitting round a table.

A short, fat man with an American accent was speaking.

"OK, so this is... what we know. Texas Airlines flight TX1068 crashed during a thunderstorm at 10.35, London time, on 6th May. The flight recorder has been checked, but it seems there was nothing wrong with the plane.

"No bodies were found on the plane, not even the pilot or flight crew. Twelve hours after the crash, some of the passengers started turning up in different parts of the world - China, Australia, Peru, Alaska.

"Only passengers aged between eight and sixteen have been found. Twenty of them have reappeared so far. They all tell the same story. They remember nothing about the flight, or what happened to them after the crash. They all seem unharmed, as far as we can tell.

"So where do we go from here?"

"We need to find out a number of things. What has happened to the missing passengers and crew? What happened to these young people during the twelve hours they were missing? How is it possible for them to turn up on the other side of the world?"

A woman in a blue uniform spoke. "I think there's one more thing we need to think about."

"What's that?"

"Are the kids that returned the same ones that disappeared? Or do they just look the same?"

"What are you getting at?"

"Human beings can't just disappear then turn up somewhere else. So what I am asking is - are they still human beings?"

CHAPTER 4
Who Are You?

The flight home from Australia was very long. Gemma had been very worried about how Becky would cope with it.

The twins didn't remember the crash, but had read about it in the newspapers. They had spent hours being interviewed.

Becky hated flying even before all this had happened. How would she cope?

They were shown to their places on the plane. They were flying first class.

The girls stretched back on the huge seats.

"Don't worry Becky, it can't happen again," Gemma whispered to her sister.

Becky smiled at her sister.
"I'm not worried! I'm just looking forward to travelling first class!"

The seatbelt light went off. Becky looked round.
"Hey!" she called to a flight attendant.
"How about some drinks then!"

Twenty-three hours later, the plane touched down. Gemma and Becky were rushed to a special room, away from reporters, to meet their parents.

Gemma was quiet on the drive home, but Becky wanted to talk. She told her parents all about the holiday in Texas. It was as if nothing had happened.

That night, Gemma woke up. She and Becky were closer than any two people could be. She knew that something was very wrong.

She got up and went into her sister's room. Becky was wide awake, reading a magazine.

Gemma looked her straight in the face. Now she was sure.
"Who are you?" she said.

Becky looked up.

"What do you mean? Don't you know who I am?"

"Not any more. Becky, you've . . . changed."

"Hasn't it changed you then?" asked Becky.

She looked carefully at her sister. "You're right!" she said. "You're still the same old Gemma. And what are we going to do about that?"

CHAPTER 5
Twins Are Special

The next day Gemma went for a walk by herself. She wanted to think things through.

There was a hill behind the house, with a clump of trees at the top. Gemma climbed the hill. At the top, she sat on a fallen branch.

"I knew I would find you here."

Gemma spun round. It was Becky. Or was it?

"You don't remember anything, do you?" she said. "The big ship in the sky. What we did to you. Don't you remember when we put that thing in your head?"

Gemma just shook her head.

"It doesn't work for everyone," said Becky. "And that makes you dangerous. It means I am going to have to kill you."

Becky was still smiling when she stepped forward. A strange light seemed to be coming from her eyes.

"Becky! Don't be silly! It's me, Gemma! Your sister!"

"I know who you are. You're Gemma, and you used to be my sister."

Becky put her hands on both sides of Gemma's head. Gemma felt herself getting dizzy. She tried to push Becky away.

She stared into her eyes, and deep down she saw someone she knew. Becky! The real Becky! She was still in there, somewhere!

"Becky, you can't do this!"

Gemma slowly felt her mind clearing.

She hugged her sister. The light
coming from Becky's eyes faded away.

Becky's body started shaking. She slid
to the ground. For an awful moment
Gemma thought she was dead. But at
last Becky opened her eyes, and this
time it really was Becky.

Whatever had taken her over had gone.
Together, they had killed it. But how?

Arm in arm, they walked back down
the hill. At last Becky spoke.

"It's us. We're special. I don't think they have ever met twins before. Some things are even more powerful than they are. Gemma, everything's going to be OK!"

But across the world eighteen young people, survivors of the crash, were getting ready. A strange light was shining from their eyes.

They had a big job to do.
But soon the planet
would be theirs.

TWINS

In this story, Gemma and Becky are identical twins.
This made it difficult for the illustrator to show which was which! Can you 'spot the difference' between the two girls?

Do twins always look the same?
Not always. Twins that do are called identical twins, like Gemma and Becky in the story.

Is there any other way you can get twins?
Clones are animals grown from cells of another animal.
They will be identical to the animal they are cloned from.
The first ever cloned animal was Dolly the sheep, born in 1996.

How can you tell identical twins apart?

Twins might look exactly the same, but they always have different fingerprints. If one twin commits a crime, it's no use saying it was their twin that did it!

Are twins special?

Becky and Gemma are special! Some people think that twins can share thoughts. They say that if one twin is hurt, or in trouble, the other twin will know about it even if they are a long way apart.

QUESTIONS

- *What do you think happened to the passengers on the plane?*

- *What did the woman in the blue uniform want to find out? What do you think is the answer to her question?*

- *Gemma thought that Becky had changed after the crash. In what ways had she changed?*

- *Why do you think Becky needed to kill Gemma?*

- *If the author wrote a sequel to this story, what would happen in it?*